San Francisco
ABC

A Larry Gets Lost book

Written and Illustrated by
John Skewes

little bigfoot

an imprint of sasquatch books
seattle, wa

ABCDEFGHI

Manufactured in China by C&C Offset Printing Co. Ltd. Shenzhen, Guangdong Province, in November 2015

Published by Little Bigfoot, an imprint of Sasquatch Books
20 19 18 17 16   9 8 7 6 5 4 3 2 1

Editor: Susan Roxborough
Production editor: Em Gale
Design: Mint Design
Interior composition: Joyce Hwang

Library of Congress Cataloging-in-Publication Data is available.

ISBN: 978-1-57061-994-6

Sasquatch Books
1904 Third Avenue, Suite 710
Seattle, WA 98101
(206) 467-4300
www.sasquatchbooks.com
custserv@sasquatchbooks.com

This
is

And
this is

JK**L**MNO**P**QRS

Larry.

Pete.

TuVwXYz

They like looking for **letters**
as they walk down the street.

Aa

A is for **Alcatraz.**

Alcatraz Island

Bb

B

is for
Bay Bridge.

Cc

C
is for
**cable
car.**

POWELL
AND
MARKET

Meet me
at the
St. Francis

FISHERMAN'S
WHARF

The Powell Street lines

Dd

D is for **Dragon Gate.**

忠孝仁愛

義信

Ee

is for
Embarcadero.

Ff

F

is for
**Ferry
Building.**

SAN FRANCISCO

PORT OF

Gg

is for
**Golden Gate
Bridge.**

H

is for hills.

I

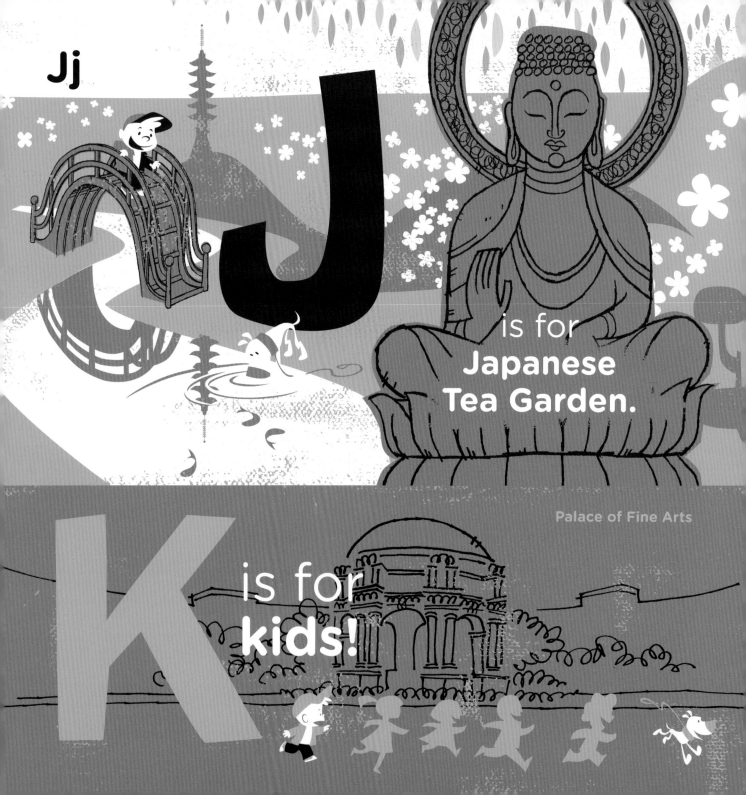

Jj

J

is for
**Japanese
Tea Garden.**

Palace of Fine Arts

K

is for
kids!

L is for Lombard Street.

Kk

Mm

M is for the **Mission.**

Nn

N is for Nob Hill.

Mission District murals

Oo

is for
ocean.

Pp

P

is for
Presidio.

Qq

Q is for **quake.**

R

Rr

R is for **rainbow.**

Ss

Tt

S

is for
sea lions.

T
is for
Transamerica Pyramid.

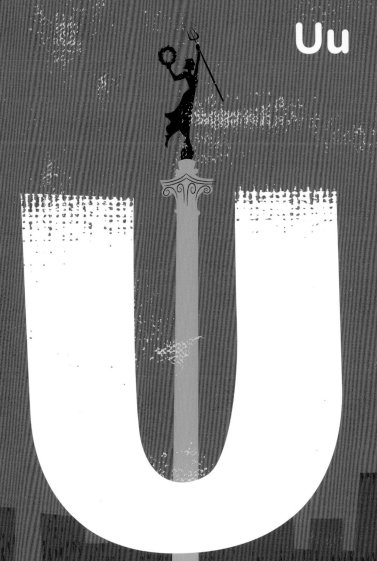

U
is for
Union Square.

V is for

VAN
1700

Ww

W

FISHERMAN'S WHARF · OF SAN FRANCISCO

Tarantino's

RESTAU

Tarantin

GUARDINO'S

SABELLA/LATORRE

NICK'S

Fisherman's Wharf

NESS

Vv

Van Ness Avenue

is for **wharf.**

8 ALIOTO'S

9 Fishermen's Grotto

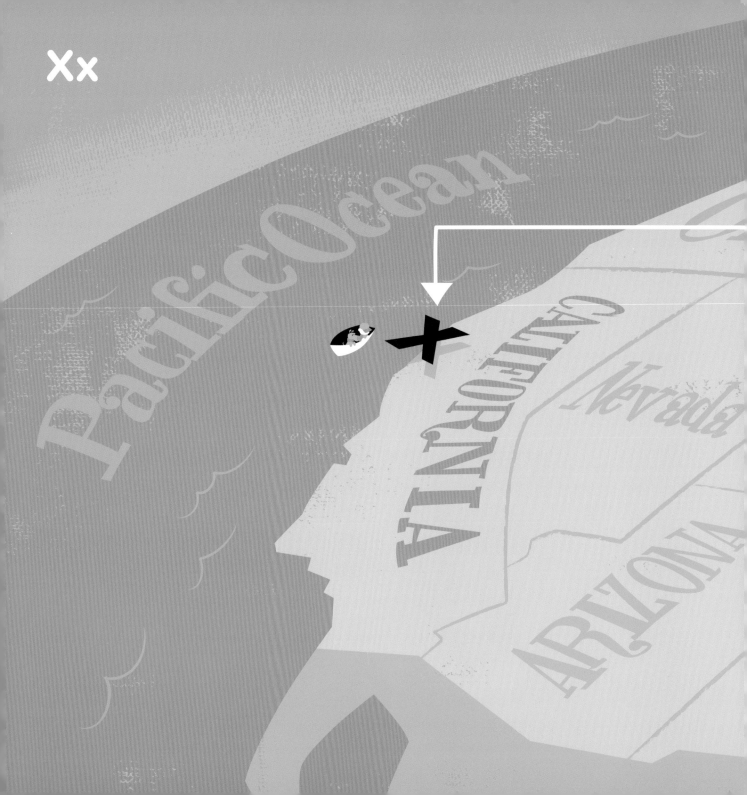

X

marks the
spot where
San Francisco is!

Y

Yy

is for
de **Young**
Museum.

Zz

and

Z

San Francisco Zoo & Gardens

is for **ZOO.**

A B C D E F
G H I J K L
M N O P Q
R S T U V
W X Y Z

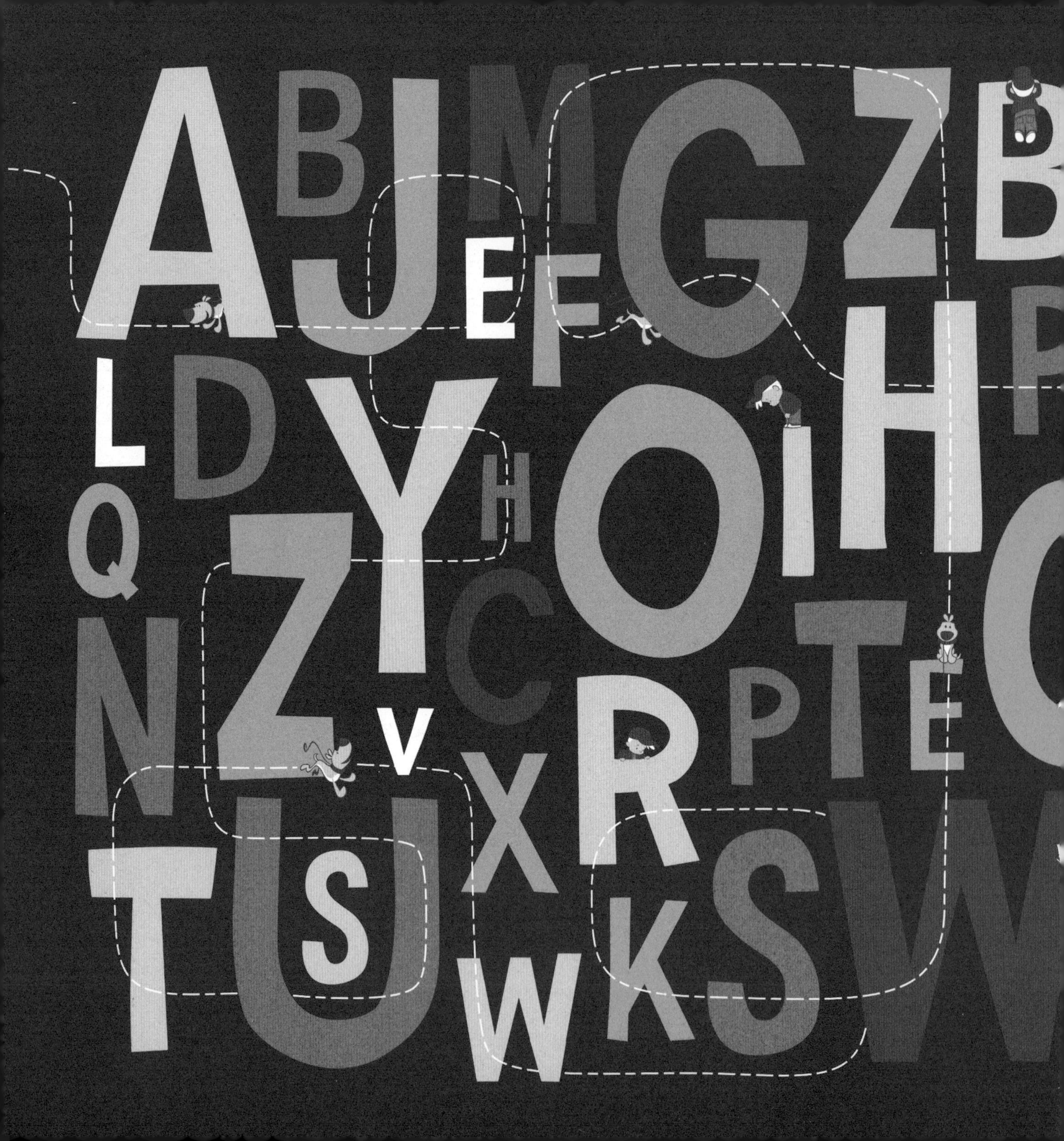